D0852647

WITHDRAWN
FROM THE RECORDS OF THE
MID-CONTINENT PUBLIC LIBRARY

JF
Avery, Ben.
Pyramid peril

MID-CONTINENT PUBLIC LIBRARY
Liberty Branch
1000 Kent Street
Liberty, MO 64068

LI

PYRAMID
PERIL

Pyramid Peril
Copyright © 2007 by Ben Avery
Illustrations copyright © 2007 by Adi Darda Guadiamo

Requests for information should be addressed to:

Zondervan, Grand Rapids, Michigan 49530

Library of Congress Cataloging-in-Publication Data

Avery, Ben, 1974–
    Pyramid Peril / by Ben Avery; art by Adi Darda
        p. cm. -- (TimeFlyz; #01)
        Includes bibliographical references and index.
        ISBN-13: 978-0-310-71361-6 (pbk. : alk. paper)
        ISBN-10: 0-310-71361-7 (pbk. : alk. paper)
        1. Graphic novels. I. Adi Darda, 1972- II. Title.
    PN6727.A945P97 2007
    741.5'973--dc22

                            2007003754

All Scripture quotations, unless otherwise indicated, are taken from the Holy Bible: New International Version®. NIV®. Copyright © 1973, 1978, 1984 by International Bible Society. Used by permission of Zondervan. All rights reserved.

All rights reserved. No part of this publication may be reproduced, stored in a retrieval system, or transmitted in any form or by any means — electronic, mechanical, photocopy, recording, or any other — except for brief quotations in printed reviews, without the prior permission of the publisher.

Series Editor: Bud Rogers
Managing Editor: Bruce Nuffer
Managing Art Director: Merit Alderink

Printed in United States

08 09 10 • 5 4 3 2

PYRAMID PERIL

SERIES EDITOR:
BUD ROGERS

STORY BY BEN AVERY
ART BY ADI DARDA GUADIAMO

ZONDERVAN®

ZONDERVAN.com/
AUTHORTRACKER
follow your favorite authors

MID-CONTINENT PUBLIC LIBRARY
Liberty Branch
1000 Kent Street
Liberty, MO 64068

LI

MID-CONTINENT PUBLIC LIBRARY

3 0000 13181098 2

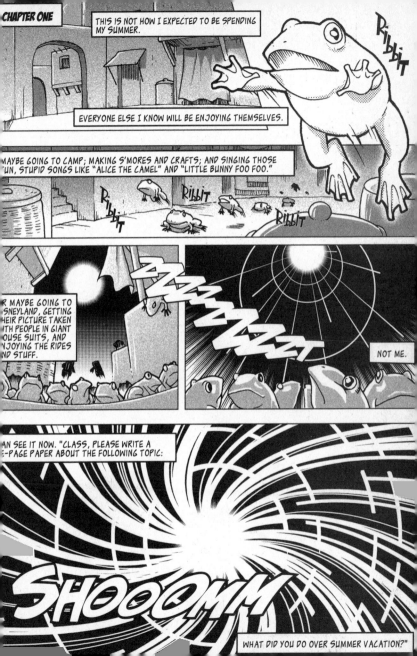

"FOR THE SUMMER HOLIDAY, I WAS KIDNAPPED BY FIVE CYBORG FLIES AND SHRUNK DOWN TO INSECT SIZE SO I COULD TRAVEL BACK IN TIME WITH THEM TO SAVE THE WORLD FROM AN EVIL SPIDER."

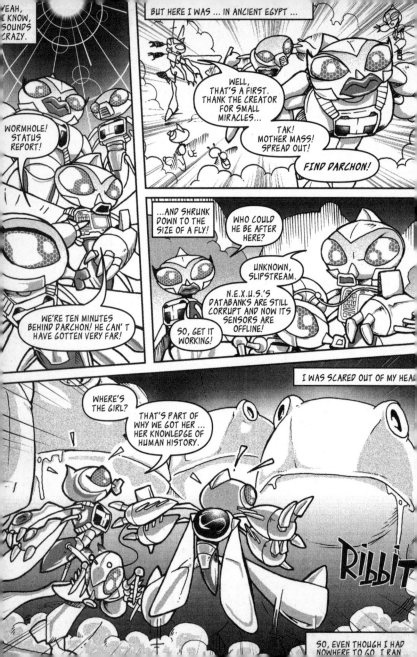

END CHAPTER ONE

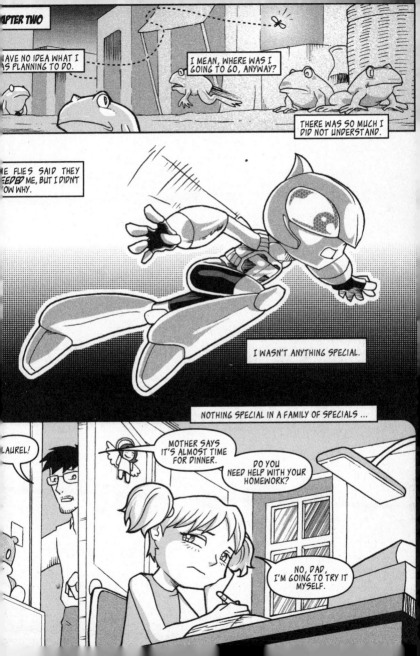

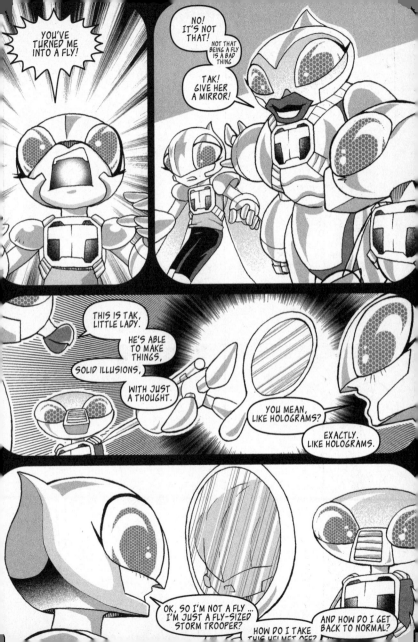

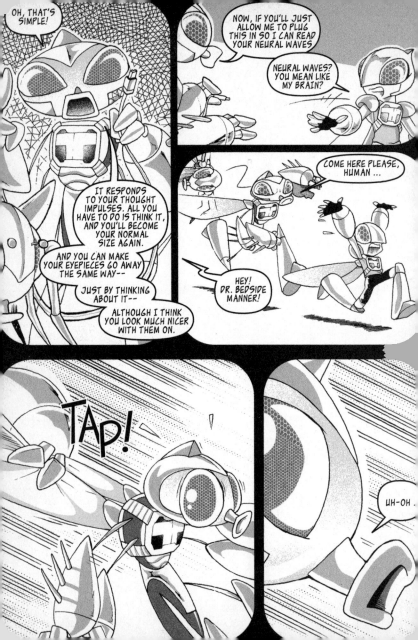

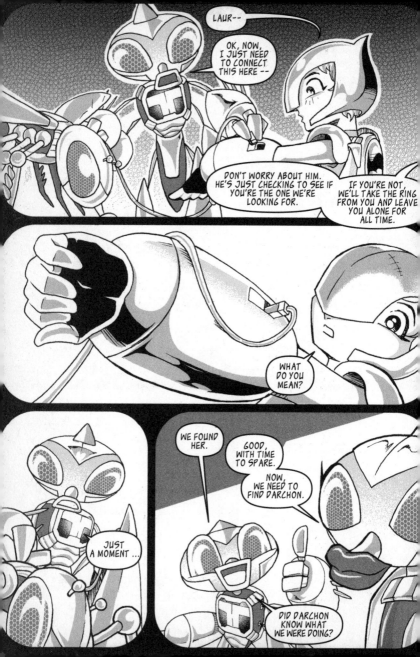

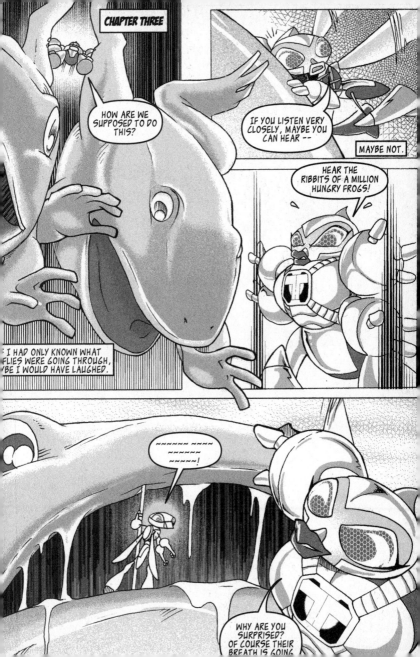

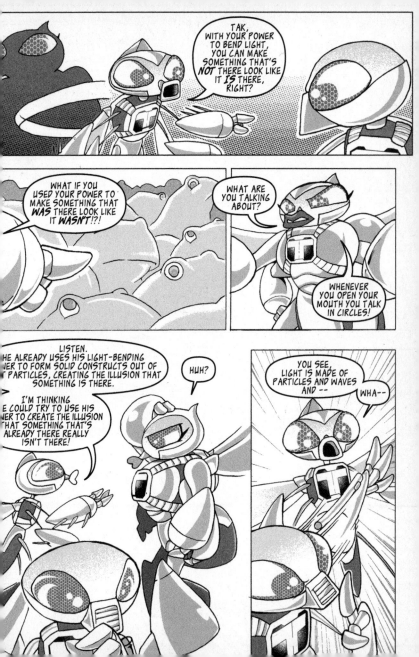

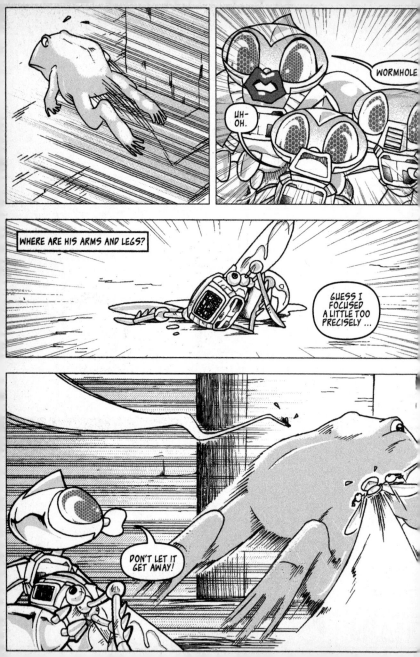

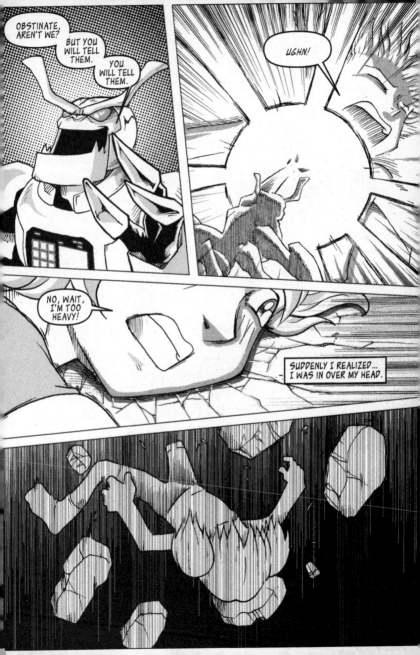

CHAPTER SIX

ALVINA.

LAUREL. LAUREL TEMPLETON.

LAUR-EL LAUR-EL TEMPLE-TON.

ST CALL LAUREL.

LAUREL.

LAUREL?

HOW LONG WAS I OUT?

I DON'T REMEMBER ANYTHING.

I FEEL JUST FINE!

REALLY, I'M GREAT!

TICHLI· AT CHADEDET LE'ECHOL·

I'M JUST ...

I'M SORRY ...

IT'S NOT THE SOUP ...

THERE'S A LOT GOING ON ... FLIES ... SPIDERS ... SHRINKING ... GROWING ...

I FEEL LIKE ALICE IN WONDERLAND!

TISHANI POH AT TZEMICHA LANU'ACH.

THANK YOU ...

AT BRIVAH?

AT GAM XEN SHHFCHAH?

HMM XEFAR ACHER ULA?

I'M SORRY, I CAN'T UNDERSTAND YOU ...

UH, MAY I PLEASE ...

MMM, MMMH, GOOD!

I COULDN'T COMMUNICATE MUCH WITH ALVINA.

WE TAUGHT EACH OTHER OUR NAMES AND THAT WAS ABOUT IT.

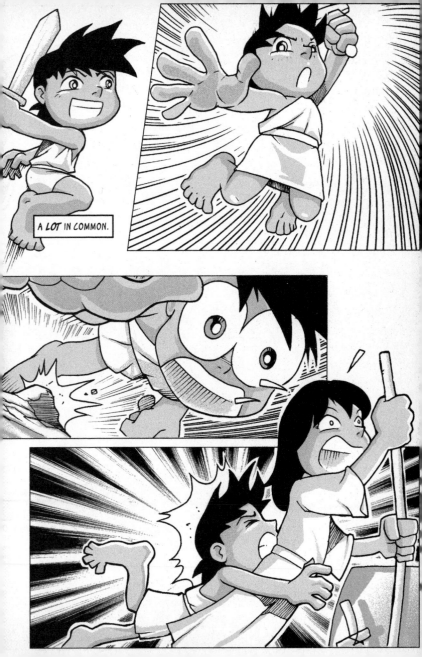

A *LOT* IN COMMON.

BUT I WAS STILL AN OUTSIDER.

HE LOVES YOU GUYS VERY MUCH ...

IT'LL BE OK, ALVINA ...

ALVINA?

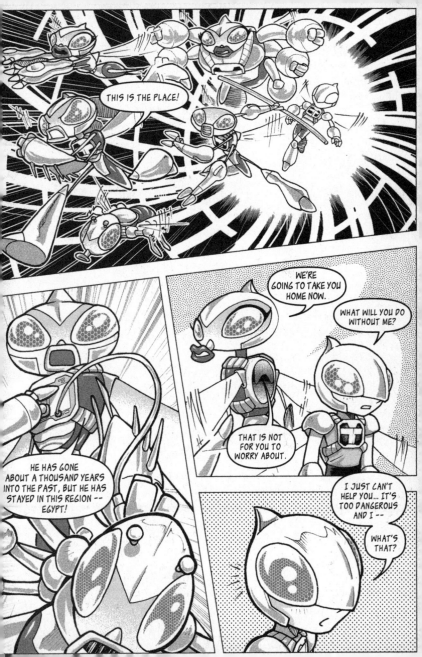

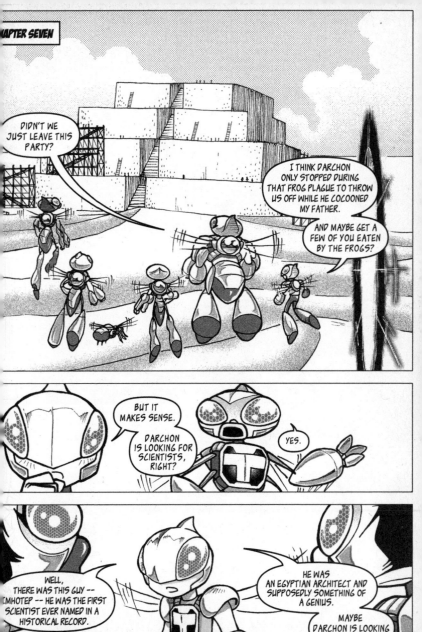

CHAPTER SEVEN

LITTLE MISS MUFFET SAT ON HER TUFFET EATING HER CURDS AND WHEY ...

ALONG CAME A SPIDER ...

WE FAILED ...

I FAILED.

REALLY?

YOU HELPED SAVE DOZENS OF LIVES --

AND WE'VE NEVER BEEN THIS CLOSE TO CATCHING DARCHON -- NOT UNTIL YOU WERE HELPING US.

FROM THE READINGS I'M GETTING, IT LOOKS LIKE DARCHON IS HEADING INTO THE FUTURE ABOUT 4,000 YEARS!

WAIT!

SHOOOMM

I'M GOING TO HELP YOU, BUT THERE'S SOMETHING I WANT TO DO FIRST.

I WANT TO LEARN HEBREW AND GO SOMEWHERE -- SOMEWHEN, I GUESS -- BEFORE WE GO AFTER DARCHON AGAIN.

PLEASE?

CHAPTER EIGHT

⟨ALVINA! ALVINA!⟩*

* IN PERFECT ANCIENT HEBREW!

⟨LAUREL! YOU'RE ALIVE!⟩

⟨I THOUGHT SOMETHING TERRIBLE HAD HAPPENED TO YOU!⟩

⟨NO! I JUST HAD TO GO ... SOMEPLACE ELSE.⟩

⟨YOU ... YOU SPEAK MY TONGUE PERFECTLY ...⟩

⟨YES, I KNOW. I GUESS YOU COULD SAY I'M A QUICK STUDY.⟩

⟨I HAVE TO GO NOW, ALVINA!⟩

⟨BUT I WANTED TO THANK YOU AND SAY GOOD-BYE.⟩

⟨WHAT? NO!⟩

⟨YOU CAN'T LEAVE!⟩

CYOUR FATHER SEEMS TO BE MUCH HAPPIER TODAY!>

CHE IS!>

CALL OF US SLAVES ARE!>

CMORE STRANGE THINGS HAPPENED AFTER YOU LEFT, LAUREL!>

CFROM THE FROGS TO THE NILE TO THE STORM TO THE LOCUSTS AND OTHER BUGS ... GOD HAS SHOWN HIS TRUE POWER ...>

CAND TONIGHT-- I DON'T KNOW EXACTLY HOW --> CALL FIRSTBORN SONS ARE SUPPOSED TO DIE TONIGHT UNLESS BLOOD IS PAINTED ON THEIR DOORPOSTS.>

CALL FIRSTBORNS! EVEN THE PHARAOH'S!>

CMY FATHER SAYS EGYPT TOOK OUR SONS, AND NOW IT SEEMS THAT PHARAOH'S SON WILL BE TAKEN FROM HIM!>

CBUT NOT MY BROTHER! I'M NOT GOING TO LOSE HIM!>

CNO, I GUESS YOU WON'T...>

CIT'S ALL SO HORRIBLE AND FANTASTIC AT THE SAME TIME!>

CWELL, I KNOW YOU'RE GOING TO HAVE A GOOD TIME AS A FAMILY TONIGHT...>

THANKS!

LET'S GO!

I HATED TO SAY GOOD-BYE

EVEN THOUGH WE HADN'T BEEN ABLE TO EVEN SPEAK THE SAME LANGUAGE FOR THE FIRST HALF OF OUR FRIENDSHIP, I FELT WE WERE KINDRED SPIRITS OF SOME SORT.

UT SHE HAD HER FAMILY AND HER FRIENDS ...

... AND I HAD SOME NEW FRIENDS WHO NEEDED MY HELP!

AND I NEEDED THEIR HELP TO HELP MY FAMILY.

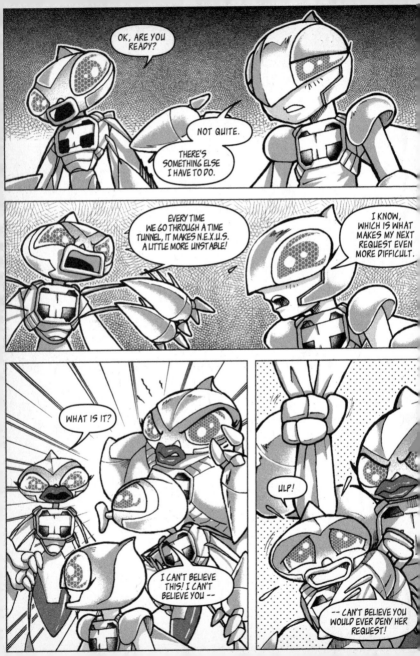